MW00951154

To Ori!
I hope you enjoy the adventure!
Paul Yalowitz

THE ADMIRAL & THE PENGUIN

words & pictures by

Paul Yalowitz

to

my wife

Polly

 Book design by Brizida Ahrnsbrak. The drawings in this book were created using graphite and color pencils on bristol vellum paper.

Paul Yalowitz, 2016
The Admiral and The Penguin, by Paul Yalowitz.
ISBN-13: 978-1533645487

Once there was an Admiral who sailed the seven seas.

But he is retired now and misses
his days of glory and adventure on
the high seas.

The Admiral discovered that the Zoo
in his city didn't have any penguins
so the Admiral decided to go on one last adventure...

ZOO: NO PENGUINS
SHIPSHAPE HOME FOR RETIRED SAILORS

The Admiral would sail to Antarctica and capture the *elusive Royal Penguin* and sell him to the zoo.

The Admiral booked passage on a ship and was very excited when the expedition began. The voyage to Antarctica went smoothly and without incident.

SS "AUNT" ARCTIC

Soon after arriving in Antarctica
the Admiral captured the *elusive Royal Penguin*.

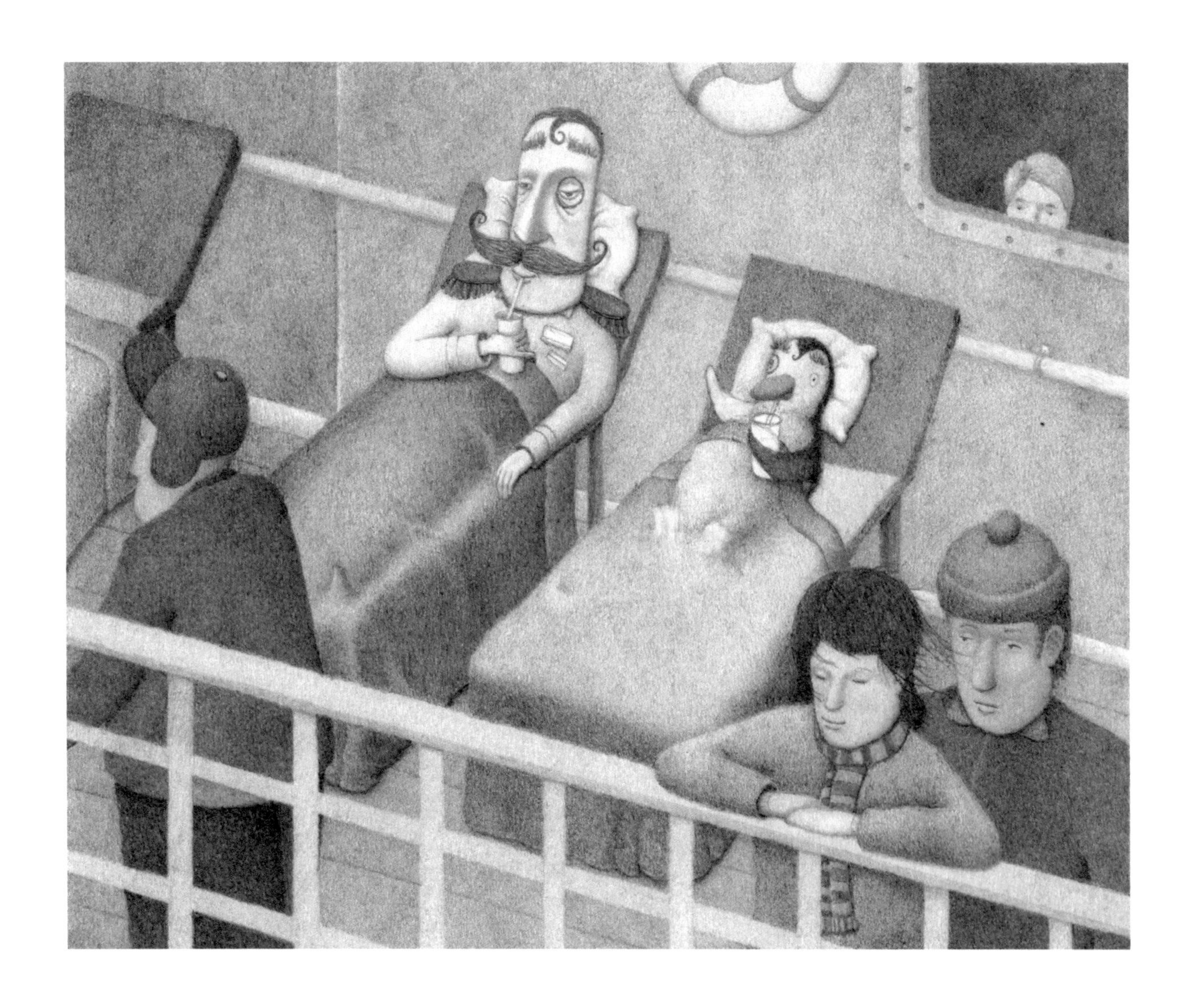

With the Admiral and the *elusive Royal Penguin* safely on board, the ship set off to return home.

On the voyage home the ship hit an iceberg and sank.

The Admiral and the *elusive Royal Penguin* found themselves stranded on the very iceberg that sunk the ship. The Admiral thought all was lost and this would be the end of his adventurous life.

The elusive Royal Penguin caught fish for the Admiral to eat. Soon they were both rescued. (actually, the *elusive Royal Penguin* didn't really need rescuing as much as the Admiral did).

Even though the *elusive Royal Penguin*
saved the Admiral's life...

CITY
City Zoo
PAY TO THE ORDER OF
THE ADMIRA
DATE
One Hundred
MEMO for Penguin

The Admiral still sold the *elusive Royal Penguin* to the Zoo. Then he wrote a book about his exciting adventure and became rich and famous.

On the first anniversary
of receiving *the elusive
Royal Penguin*, the Zoo
had a big celebration
and invited the Admiral
back for a reunion.
When the Admiral saw
the *elusive Royal Penguin*
he became quite dismayed.
The *elusive Royal Penguin*
was very thin and
appeared sad, sickly
and depressed.
The admiral immediately
had a change of heart...

he thought,

"What did I do? For my own glory I have ruined this poor bird's life."

The Admiral offered to buy the *elusive Royal Penguin* back from the Zoo so he could return the bird to his home, but the Zoo refused to sell him because the *elusive Royal Penguin* was a popular attraction. That night the Admiral came up with a plan – yet another last adventure...

Admiral
Penguin
Zoo
109

The next night, the Admiral snuck into the Zoo and took the *elusive Royal Penguin* in order to return him home to Antarctica.

They made it all the way to
the docks before the Police
caught up with them.
But, before the Admiral
was captured and arrested,
the *elusive Royal Penguin*
managed to escape into
the water.
He was elusive after all.

The Admiral was put on trial and found guilty of stealing the *elusive Royal Penguin*; he lost all his money and popularity.

ADMIRAL
AND THE PENGUIN
THE BADMIRAL
AND THE PENGUIN
GUILTY
GUILTY
GUILTY
GUILTY

LOCKEM UPUS
CITY
JAIL
INSECURE
BIRD SONGS

The Admiral was sent to jail for a short time, but he was the happiest he had ever been, because he knew that even though he didn't get to return the *elusive Royal Penguin* home at least he gave him his freedom back. While the admiral was in jail, every morning on his windowsill, he would find...

a fish.

the end

CPSIA information can be obtained at www.ICGtesting.com
Printed in the USA
LVIW01n2341181016
509353LV00005B/13